·A Twin Tales Storybook·

Cinderella

© 1994 Grandreams Limited

Published by
Grandreams Limited
Jadwin House, 205/211 Kentish Town Road,
London, NW5 2JU.

Printed in Italy

Once upon a time, there lived a rich merchant who was married to a lovely wife. They had one child, a daughter. Sadly, the wife became ill and died, leaving the merchant to look after their daughter.

After several years, the merchant married again, wanting to give his daughter a new mother. His new wife was very vain and selfish. She had been married before as well, and had two daughters. Both were extremely ugly and therefore jealous of their new stepsister who was very pretty.

A short while after they were married, the merchant died. This left his daughter all alone in the world, for her new stepmother did not love her.

The stepmother and stepsisters wasted no time.

"You will work for us from now on," they told

her. "As your father's new family, it is only right that everything he had should belong to us."

All the servants were sent away, and the daughter was made to do all the work. She had to cook, clean, mend, wash the floors and keep the fires going. They called her Cinderella.

One day an invitation arrived from the palace. The King and Queen had decided that it was time that their eldest son found a bride, and so they were holding a grand ball for all the eligible young ladies in the kingdom.

"Oh, mother," said the stepsisters. "Surely he will choose one of us, if we are in our finest dresses."

"Of course, my dears," said their mother. "Cinderella! Get to work on the finest ballgowns for my two darling daughters. The Prince is to choose a bride, and will surely choose one of them."

"Am I invited?" asked Cinderella.

"You!" declared the stepmother. "Most certainly not. Young ladies only, not servants, are invited."

Sadly, Cinderella started to work on the dresses for her stepsisters.

On the evening of the ball, the two stepsisters were dressed and ready, and the coach came to take them to the ball. Cinderella had tried very hard to make the stepsisters look attractive, but it was very difficult as they were so ugly.

Cinderella sat by the kitchen fire, wishing she could go to the ball.

"And so you shall," said a voice behind her. "I'm your fairy godmother. Find a rat, four white mice, two green frogs and a big pumpkin."

Cinderella did as she was told. She put the things in front of her fairy godmother, who waved a wand. Suddenly there appeared a beautiful coach and horses, with footmen and driver.

"And you can wear this, my dear," she turned and said. Cinderella suddenly found herself in a beautiful gown.

"Have a lovely time at the ball," said the

godmother, helping
Cinderella into the coach.

"But remember, the magic will only last until midnight."

"Thank you!" called Cinderella, as the coach sped off.

At the ball, the Prince had eyes for nobody but the beautiful stranger who would not give her name. Of course, it was Cinderella.

He danced with her all night long, and insisted that she sat by him for the banquet.

People at the ball talked endlessly of the beautiful girl who had captured the Prince's heart.

They all believed she was a Princess.

"Who is she?" said the stepsisters to their mother.

"I don't know," she answered, crossly. "But I don't think the Prince will be dancing with anybody else tonight."

The Prince danced only with Cinderella. He
had fallen completely in love and knew that she
was the girl he wanted to marry.

The evening passed very quickly for Cinderella, who had also fallen in love with the Prince.

As they danced, a clock began to chime.

"What time is it?" asked Cinderella, suddenly remembering the godmother's warning.

"Midnight, I believe," said the Prince.

"I must go," said Cinderella. Before the Prince could say anything or stop her, she had run out of the palace and down the steps. As she ran, she lost her shoe.

This was all the Prince found. Guards at the gate said all they had seen was a dirty servant girl, not a beautiful Princess.

The Prince was very sad. He declared that he would search the kingdom until he found the girl who could wear the shoe he had found.

The Prince visited every girl who had been at the ball. Eventually he came to the merchant's house.

The two ugly sisters fought to try the shoe on, but it was far too small.

Cinderella came into the room, and was told to try on the shoe. Of course, it fitted beautifully.

The happy Prince married Cinderella.

Beauty And The Beast

Once upon a time, there lived a very wealthy merchant. He and his family had everything they could possibly need, and lived in a beautiful mansion.

One day, the merchant had some bad news. Two of his ships had been sunk in a storm, and a third was missing. He had lost everything.

The merchant sold his mansion, and his daughters' jewels to pay off his debts. Then the family had to move to a tiny cottage by a forest.

Two of his daughters found it very hard, and complained all day long. His youngest daughter worked hard, trying to make a new home for her father, and was often found working in her vegetable garden, or doing the cleaning or cooking.

Several months passed, and one day a messenger came to the cottage.

"I have good news for you," he said.

The merchant listened as the messenger told him that the third ship had finally limped into port, with a full cargo. Much of the merchant's fortune was restored.

"I must go and sort out the matter," he told his daughters. "What gift would you like me to bring home for you?"

The two older girls chose silks and satins.

"Bring me a rose, father," said Beauty.

The merchant travelled to town, and completed his affairs. He bought the gifts for his daughters and then tried to buy a rose for Beauty, but there were none to be had.

It was late when he left, still without a rose, and he travelled through the unfamiliar country in the dark. He saw some lights in the distance, and found a beautiful mansion.

Food was laid on for him by unseen servants, and a bed was prepared. He did not see his host.

The following morning, he prepared to leave, but then saw the garden. It was full of roses.

"Beauty's present," he said, as he picked one.

"How dare you!" roared a voice behind him. The merchant turned to see the most ugly creature he had ever seen.

"Bring me the first thing you see, when you arrive home," said the Beast.

The merchant was terrifed and agreed, certain it would be his dog. It was Beauty who ran to greet him. The merchant told her what had happened.

"Of course I will go," said Beauty. But when she met the Beast in his garden she was shocked by how ugly he was.

The merchant said farewell to his daughter, and left her at the Beast's mansion.

The Beast was very kind to Beauty and she had all she could possibly need.

She soon grew used to the Beast, and looked forward to their time together.

After a few months, the Beast asked her a question.

"Do you love me?"

"No," said Beauty. "But I like you."

One day, the Beast gave Beauty a mirror so that she could see her family when she wished.

Beauty was very happy and after a while did not look at it for a few months.

When she did look, what she saw made her very upset. Her father was lying in bed, very ill.

Beauty ran to find the Beast.

"Please let me go home," she cried. "My father is very ill. I must see him."

The Beast agreed, and gave her a ring. "If it is shiny, I am well," he told her. "If it is dull, I am dying."

Beauty was taken back to her father's home in one of the Beast's fine carriages. The merchant had been very ill, but he cheered up considerably when he saw his daughter.

The summer months passed, and the merchant grew stronger.

"When you are well, I must return," Beauty told her father.

"Surely he won't mind if you stay a little longer," said the merchant. "Until I am really strong."

Summer passed into autumn, and in no time Christmas was upon them.

"I must go back," said Beauty.

"Surely not at Christmas," said the merchant. "Stay just until the spring. I will be really fit and well then."

Beauty agreed. Christmas was very happy, and the snows came just after, so travelling was impossible.

Nearly six months had passed, and the merchant was nearly fully recovered. He was very happy to have Beauty at home with him.

One day, in early spring, Beauty was going through some drawers.

Tucked away, at the back, was the ring the Beast had given her. She had put it in a box in the drawer for safe keeping. She had looked at it faithfully every day for the first couple of months, but then it had been gradually pushed to the back of the drawer.

She opened the box, and cried out. The ring was completely dull. The Beast was dying! He may already be dead.

She ran to find her father, and with tears in her eyes, told him about the ring.

"I must go back to him," she cried. "He might already be dead."

The merchant immediately called for a carriage to take his daughter back to the Beast's mansion.

She leapt out of the carriage, and ran up the

drive to the house. She ran from room to room, searching for the Beast.

Then she went outside and headed for the beautiful rose garden, where she saw him lying on the ground.

"Don't die," she cried. "I love you."

A sudden flash knocked her to the ground.

"Ah, Beauty, you've broken the spell," said the Beast. And he turned around. It was a handsome young man.

Beauty and her Beast were married.